I T C H

A Novella

Ash Ericmore

Special thanks to Corrina and No Remorse Reviews for the undying support and the back cover image. ☺

C H A P T E R   1

You have to be kidding me. Bobby wanted to fuck. For fuck's sake. *Wait.* That didn't come out right. He usually only wanted it every few weeks these days. Janie sat on the edge of the bed listening to the sound of the shower. At least that was thoughtful of him. To wash first. Fuck. Well. Never mind. She'd thought that the new Playstation coming out would deter him for a few days. Maybe even a week. Especially if one of those war game duty things was on the release schedule. MMOGTFO's or whatever.

But no. He wanted to fuck.

She pulled the collar of her t-shirt away from her skin and looked down the inside. She didn't want to. Not really. Not like she *used* to want to. Especially not having just puked a little while ago. *Again.* She was beginning to think she was coming down with something. She looked at the door. She should run for it. Don't give him the satisfaction. But he'd only follow her. She should leave him. Tell him that she didn't want him anymore. But he'd only follow her. Like he always did.

That one time. The time she'd met a guy call Alfie—stupid fucking name, mind—down the pub on her lunch break from work. He was nice. Sweet. He didn't talk down to her. He didn't treat her like she was a second hand citizen in her own home. She'd agreed to meet up with him the next day, same time, same pub. Three days (dates if you will) into that friendship, and Bobby had turned up. One of his mates must have seen her talking to this simple, harmless dude. The two of them had been sitting at one of the tables in the corner and Bobby had walked in and grabbed a pool cue from the stand by the table.

Neither of them had seen him coming. Wrapped up in each other's company, she supposed.

Anyway. Bobby did what Bobby did. He brought the thick end of the cue down on the back of Alfie's shoulders. Hurt, you see. Really fucking hurt. He was good at that sort of thing. It didn't so much as scratch the cue. It left no visible marks on the face. But it felt like someone had stabbed you in the back. It took your breath completely away. Stole it, refusing to give it back. Bruised the bones. But they were solid bones back there. It didn't break anything. It just made it impossible to sit back for a week. You couldn't lay on your back because it hurt so much. And that was the point. It was a warning.

He'd done to Janie once. That was how she knew.

Anyway. She never saw Alfie again. Which was the point, she supposed.

She wished she was with Alfie now, wherever he was. She had tried going back to the pub again. Even after work. She asked at the bar. They said they thought they knew who she was talking about, but they hadn't seen him for a few days ... then weeks, before she gave up.

The shower stopped.

Oh well. Janie shuffled her bum back up the bed,

until she was sitting in the middle of it, her back against the headboard. She should make it nice for him. Then he'd finish quicker. She heard the door to the bathroom open and the padding of his feet. He came straight to the bedroom. Knew she'd be there. He just had a towel wrapped around his waist. Wasn't even properly dried. He smiled at her, but didn't speak. Flipped the radio on. It was stood on a bar stool in the corner of the bedroom. Bare white painted walls. Cord carpet. Bar stool for bedroom furniture. It was amazing what you thought about at times like that. *When Bobby was preparing.*

The news played on the radio. *The farm has been quarantined following further investigation*, it said. That sounded interesting, but Bobby flicked the switch to play a CD. It autoplayed the one in there. She didn't know what it was, but it was loud guitars and heavy drums. The sort of music where you couldn't understand the vocalist (if you could call him that) as he screamed like he was vomiting into the microphone.

Bobby waited for the music to start. He bopped his head forward a few times, and strode into the middle of the room like he owned the place. She paid the fucking rent. He dropped the towel. Luckily his cock wasn't particularly big so he didn't hurt her with it.

Although she screamed sometimes.

He liked that.

It was already at half-mast. She made cooing sounds and he approached the bed. She pulled her skirt up over her waist. She wasn't wearing any knickers. Spread her legs. Hopefully she could get this done with a quickie. "I want you to fuck me," she said. "Now. Do it now." His cock got harder.

Thank fuck for that.

He got on the bed and crawled up to her. He jammed his fucking fingers at her, banging around, not knowing what he was doing. Not caring. He wanted to finger fuck her first, and didn't care what she wanted. Or felt. She let out a little yelp as he prodded her once too often, not only failing to finding the target, but not concerned with whether she had any sort of lubrication or not. She took his hand and guided him in the right direction. She knew not to try and dissuade him. It would hurt less that way.

But as soon as she tried to help, he tired of the idea, and got up on his knees. Cock waving at her. "Suck me," he said.

Okay. She could do that.

CHAPTER 2

Janie lay on her front with her face buried in the pillow. He'd only decided in the end he did actually want to fuck her. Fucking hell. He was at it now. Ploughing—she was sure he would say—the shit out of her. In all fairness, she could feel him. But wasn't exactly feeling *the plough*. He was grunting away— all of ninety seconds into his athletic bout of astonishing love-making—and about to cum.

She felt him when he did. Wasn't wearing a johnny, of course. He wanted to say that he liked to go commando to his friends, but in all truth, by the time she'd put the thing on him, he was usually pretty close to finishing. So that went out the window.

He rolled off her and onto the bed next to her. He was huffing away like he'd run a fucking marathon. Fucker. "That was great," she said, rolling out of the damp spot. She pulled her skirt down, re-dressing in record time. He was completely naked. He wiped his dick on the sheets. Nice. He didn't even say he'd had a nice time. Nothing. Janie stared at the ceiling in thought. He had rather seemed to have gone off it these days. Maybe it was her? Maybe he was growing out of her? Fat fucking chance.

He sat up, swung his legs off the bed and went over to the pile of clothes by the wall. He pulled out a pair of boxer shorts—that weren't clean when he tossed them down there—and pulled them on. She resisted asking if he was going to bother to shower.

Because he wasn't. Not twice in one day. Then he left the room without saying a word to her.

She waited there, listening. She wanted to know what he was up to before she decided on her next move. He slammed the door to the living room and she heard the Playstation fire up. Then she could hear him, almost immediately. Talking to someone on chat. He was saying he'd just scored with his hot girlfriend. She would do him if he told her to, too. *Cunt.* She got up from the bed and went to the window leaning out onto the sill.

Their bedroom window overlooked the street, there was the small garden below that belonged to the flat downstairs, then an iron fence that butted up on the path. The road was usually pretty busy. It was the main road out of this dump of a town. She watched someone cycle by, gently. It looked relaxing. She watched an older gentleman walking the pavement. A couple of cars go by. It was warm. Sometime during the week. The days all blended into each other when she wasn't at work. And a week off meant a week in the flat being pawed at by *him*.

Oh, if only the Playstation had done its job.

She watched as a man, maybe in his forties was walking along the other side of the street. He was pale. Sweaty like he'd been jogging, but he was wearing a suit. He stopped and held onto the wall for a moment, before he looked around and noticed her. She smiled at him. A quick, neighbourly affair. Just being nice. He smiled back and straightened himself. The gesture of someone who didn't want to look sickly in front of a potential mate. Then he walked towards her. Out into the road.

There was the squeal of some brakes and a car hit him. Janie was no good at cars. It was like a Mondeo, but not. Blue. Four doors. Not that she needed to know, because the car did at least stop. Well, it had to, what with the windscreen being obstructed.

The not-Mondeo was probably doing more than the speed limit. Most cars along there did. It hit the suited man low on his legs, and slid him up onto the bonnet. The impact had probably broken his legs. His whole body twisted, before going limp, just as his head hit the windscreen.

There didn't look to be much damage to his actual head, from where Janie was watching from, but by the amount of blood that sploshed across the glass, his head must have popped open like a condom full of water being tossed around. Like a water balloon. She screamed. Of course she did. She left the window and ran across the flat, through the hallway and out the front door onto the landing shouting *accident*. Bobby didn't even call out to find out what the problem was. Just shooting the people in the game.

She bounded down the stairs, and out the front of the building. There was a small gathering already. She burst through the gates, and to the side of the car. Janie put her hand over her mouth. The man's leg were mangled. Bone was jutting out of the leg of his charcoal suit somewhere near where his knee should have been. Blood was pumping from his trousers, out onto the body of the car, the blood looking black on the blue paintwork. She couldn't turn away from him, as much as she wanted to. His body was twisted at an angle that suggested his internal organs were arse about face now, and his head was dented like the bumper of the car was. As Janie's gaze moved up his body, she realised he was staring back at her, one eye misted out and white. And in there, somewhere, was a small spark of life.

He wasn't dead.

The people around her were at a hush, and no one was acknowledging that he was still there, in more than just spirit. Fuck. She needed to do something.

Then he moved.

That fucking woke everyone else up.

There was shuffling and screaming. *Oh my God,* they were saying, *somebody help him.* But Janie watched him move. He was pulling his arm down from above his head, twisted, his wrist corkscrewed around. Shards of glass from the windscreen jabbed into it, sticking out, blood weeping from the wounds. He slid it down to beside his body. The crowd all made noises, but no one approached him. They all stood and stared like a deer, watching a car coming towards them. His hand flopped loose from the wrist, nerve endings slashed. Bones shattered.

And still he maintain eye contact with Janie.

His hand, blood streaked and broken, wobbled at the end of his arm, as he pushed it down to the waist of his trousers. He used his thumb to hook into them, and pulled his trousers away from his body, slipping his hand into them. Into his trousers.

He doesn't know what he's doing, one of the crowd said.

Janie could see him, moving. See the lump in his trousers as he started to move back and forth. Still staring at her. Broken. Bleeding. She took a step back. Some silly bitch screamed. Why should she care? The fucker was staring at her, at Janie. No one else. Bleeding out, and still pleasuring himself over her. She was suddenly more than aware that she wasn't wearing any knickers.

She still had dried—drying—spunk on her legs.

Jesus fucking Christ, no.

As she stepped back, the crowd closed the gap between her and the car, like Moses letting the waves return. Then she couldn't see him. He couldn't see her. She heard someone ask, *what's he doing?*

Having a wank. That's what he was doing. It was what he wanted to do. On his deathbed. Deathcar. Whatever. While looking at *her*.

CHAPTER 3

Janie left the scene of the crash, walking down the road, away from it. She didn't want to go back into the flat. To Bobby. She wanted to walk. It was a nice enough day, besides. Bare armed, wearing only a pair of flip flops she started down the path. Turned off the main road and into the estate behind. There were some shops in the middle of it. A ten minute walk. Enough time to clear her head, for sure.

Enough time to ponder what had happened. She wished she'd had her mobile with her, then she could call Dawn and talk to her about it. Fucking freaky weirdo, that bloke was. She shuddered. She left the path and crossed the road to the other side. Almost as soon as she had left the main road, the streets narrowed. Kids played in them. There were houses on both sides, facing each other. Cars parked half on and half off the path. Not many of the houses had driveways. Front gardens were tiny. A premium.

But that did mean you could usually see into people houses if you wanted. Just a cheeky glance as you walked passed. See what they were watching on TV. That sort of thing. Nothing weird. Perverted.

Well, Bobby probably did the perverted sort of gazing. But not her. She was a good girl. She wrapped her arms around herself as she walked. The t-shirt short skirt ensemble she was wearing was fine for the weather, but she did feel a little … exposed. Probably the lack of knickers.

She looked into the house she was passing. A couple of heads protruded from above the back of the sofa facing the wall mounted TV. She couldn't tell how old they were, just that they were watching a daytime soap. Some shit like Doctors. The next house had the curtains drawn. Fine.

Janie crossed at the small roundabout and over, the shops were on the corner. She didn't have any money, but that didn't matter. She knew the people that worked most shifts in most of the shops, and they wouldn't mind her doing some window shopping, or getting something on tick. They'd done it before. They all knew that she worked and she was good for it.

No idea if the owners would feel the same way. Not her problem really. She could see the Spar shop along the road. There was a Co-op next to it. She wasn't as welcome in there, but then, that was a corporation. Probably had to balance the tills and such. Not so easy to get tick in those sort of places. There was the pub, of course. The owners in there—nice couple—Donnie and Diane, they would let her have one on her tab. Janie thought that one of them—Diane, at least—suspected that Bobby knocked her about sometimes and that was why she was so nice to her.

Not a bad idea. Maybe get a pint.

Coming up on the line of shops, Janie glanced down the side of the Co-op. Usually a trash infested shit hole, on this occasion there were a couple of lads down there. Late teens, probably. They were smoking. It was unlikely to be tobacco. One of them saw her look and called out, "All right, love?" She ignored him. It was best to ignore them. They went away, if you did.

She looked in the window of the Co-op, not stopping, the place where the cashpoint should be was boarded up. Ram-raided again, she expected, then she glanced between the Spar and the pub. Drink to take home? Share with Bobby? One in the pub? Just to herself. No contest really.

Janie crossed over to the *Bag and Tennant, Free House*. She pushed the door open and stepped in. Traditional place, it was. Like it had dropped out of the eighties. For some reason, even though the cigarette ban was some fifteen years ago, long before she'd ever set foot in a pub, the place still seemed to stink of it. It had that strange rough felt over all the seats. Sort of like a school bus. The bar had stools around it, but ones that were bolted to the floor, like there had been one too many bar fights. Everything else was wood, but not classy dark wood. Light wood. Again. The eighties.

And the place was nearly always half empty.

Even in the middle of a housing estate known mostly for the high unemployment.

"You look like you've had a day." Donnie was behind the bar polishing a glass. He always seemed to be doing that. Polishing a glass. She walked over and perched herself on one of the stools, glancing around. Dead. One other person. Old Roger. He was usually in there. He'd come in and make a pint last most of the day. Least he was never any trouble, and kept to himself. It seemed like he'd retired a decade ago, and just wanted to spend his days nursing a beer.

"That I have," she replied. "There's an accident out on the main road, just outside my place. Nasty. Guy's been hit by a car. Cut up real bad."

Donnie nodded. "What can I get you?"

"Oh, nothing." She looked down at the bar. "I just came in to see how you two were doing."

Donnie snorted lightly, almost under his breath. "On the house," he said. He took the glass he was polishing and started pouring a Guinness. "How's that man of yours?" He asked. He didn't look up though.

"Fine," she said, quietly. "You know it was the weirdest thing. That guy who was hit by the car. He was staring at me when it happened. He was looking across the road to me in the window. It was like he fancied me or something."

Donnie placed the stout down on the beer towel on the bar in front of her. "You sound surprised. Good looking lass like you."

She smiled. Snorted. Snotty one. "Fuck off," she said, a little giggle. "No, it's like there was something wrong with him."

"Maybe it'll be on the news later," he said.

"What's that?" Diane came around the corner of the bar, from out the back.

"Accident on the main road. Might be fatal," Donnie replied.

"Maybe," she said. "But the news seems to be full of this thing going on at the farms out by Canterford way."

Janie supped the ale. "What's that?"

Diane stopped what she was doing and tapped the beer mats against her lips. "I don't really know. I don't think they really know. Something's only gone and killed all the sheep out at one of the farms over there. Not far away, either. What? Thirty miles away? On our doorstep. Last thing we need. I remember foot and mouth. Bird flu. Don't need another one. Anyway. How's that man of yours?"

"Fine." Janie swivelled on the stool and faced the bar again.

"Good. No troubles in the homestead then?" She continued around the bar, dispersing beer mats. She wasn't really looking for an answer. She was just digging at her. Probably.

"Nah." She waved up at the TV behind the bar. "Stick it on then. Let's see what's going on in the world."

CHAPTER 4

Janie held the pint to her lips but wasn't drinking. She was watching the TV over the rim of the glass. BBC News 24. The newscaster was saying that there was some infection coming from the animals. Something that people could catch, and that the whole area was under quarantine. That people should avoid it. That until they'd done more testing, people should stay off farmland. Just in case.

"Fucking hell," Donnie whispered. "What's the world coming to?"

Janie shook as the sound of a glass hitting the bar rang out next to her. She turned. It was Old Roger. He'd moved over and was sitting on the stool next to her. Glass drained. "I knew," he said, "something like this was afoot."

"What you talking about?" Donnie shook his head, giving a traditional *we-got-a-right-one-here* look to Diane as she crossed in front of him, returning to the back.

"I can feel it in my balls," he said.

"Hey," Donnie scolded, "not in front of a lady."

"It's all right," Janie said, holding back a grin.

"There's something rotten in the town today," Roger said. "You mark my words." He stood up and went to the door. "You mark my words," he repeated, leaving.

Janie turned back to Donnie, after watching him leave. "What the fuck?" she whispered.

Donnie shrugged. He turned back to the TV. "Football's on the other side, do you mind?" He didn't wait for an answer before flipping the channel.

Great, Janie thought. At least they were pretty to look at. She sipped her pint. No hurry to get home.

———

Half time came and went and the team in purple were winning one to nothing. No idea who they were. Didn't care much either. Janie sat on the stool, alone in the bar. She was still nursing the same beer that she'd had for the last hour. Didn't want to leave, didn't want to ask for another. No money. Fucking hell. She was going to have to leave soon.

Donnie was out the back doing something. Probably making sandwiches, or unwrapping pork pies or something, and she hadn't seen Diane for a while.

Then the TV cut out. She looked absently at the screen. The box was still working. The signal had dropped out. "Donnie," she called. "I don't give a rat's arse, but you should know your TV's gone and fucked up."

Donnie came out from the back and looked at the screen. "Shit," he muttered. He picked up the remote and jabbed at the buttons pushing the remote closer to the TV with each thumb jab. "All the channels are gone."

"What?" she said. "You want me to try?"

He stared at her. Just quickly. It said a volume about *pressing buttons better than me?*, and she decided not to pursue the question.

Then the TV flickered back to life. A red screen. "What the hell is wrong with this thing," he said, changing channels again. And again. And again.

Each channel was showing the same thing.

Then the broadcast changed. The Prime Minster. She was standing behind a podium with a curtain behind. "This is an announcement for the people of Britain," she said.

Janie glanced at Donnie and then back to the screen. "Diane," he called. "You better come take a look at this."

"There has been an outbreak of an animal pestilence in Kent, Sussex, and Lancashire. At the moment, we do not know the cause of it, however, my advisors have suggested that we move swiftly, to ensure the safety of the people." She stopped speaking, staring at the camera, but she looked like there was more.

As if she had forgotten her lines.

She was shuffling about. Beyond the podium. It was weird. Like she was scratching at herself. Janie watched. The fuck? "What's she up to?" She glanced down to Donnie and Diane, both stood watching from behind the bar, Donnie with a glass in his hand, cleaning it. Donnie's head bobbed from side to side.

"It looks like she's …" His words drifted off.

There was a scream on the TV from behind the camera and it toppled. The picture flickered as the camera hit the floor and then everything was on its side. Janie couldn't take her eyes from it. "Fucking hell," she said too quietly for anyone else to hear. "What's …" Then her words drifted off, too.

The Prime Minister came back in the shot. It was somewhat of a shock to see the Madam P.M. holding the face of a cameraman, pinching his chin to keep him from moving it away from her—not that he was trying. The two of them were smashing lips like horny teenagers on a first date. Which was not only odd because of the P.M. thing—decorum and all—but also because Madam P.M. was married, and in her late sixties. Each to their own, but none of it seemed right somehow. Suddenly the camera's view of the two of them was blocked by another woman who Janie didn't recognise, falling in front of it. She could only see the woman's torso, but she knew it was a woman because she wasn't wearing any clothes.

"The fuck?" Diane shouted. "This shit?"

Janie tore her eyes from the TV and glanced at Diane. It was most unusual for her to swear. Looking back at the TV, the woman was rocking back and forth. She was voluptuous, and her tits were rocking like someone was fucking her off camera. Which, of course, they couldn't be, because they were in a TV studio. Obviously.

The transmission stopped and the picture on the TV returned to the red background.

"Okay," Janie said. "What the fuck was that?"

Donnie was staring at the screen, unmoved. He had the glass in one hand and a rag in the other, the two things touching, and his mouth was open, slightly. "Huh," he said.

"Politics," Diane said.

"Yes," Donnie agreed.

"I suppose I should go," Janie said, quietly. "See what's for dinner." *Not a lot*, she thought. Not much in. Order a takeaway, she supposed. She picked up her glass and supped the last of the pint down, before standing to leave. The dried cum on her legs was chaffing a bit, and she wished that she hadn't left in such a hurry now. That, and Bobby was probably going to be pissed at her for not coming back in sooner. He would want to show her his amazing kills on the killing game. Whatever it was called.

She took a step backwards towards the door. Something in the back of her mind was telling her that perhaps she should wait there for a little while.

Then the TV changed back to the football.

And Janie took a step closer to the screen.

The camera was on one of those wide shots, where you could see some of the pitch, the crowd. Good for those long passing shots. That was about the extent of Janie's knowledge of the game. The shot was stationary, and there were players on the pitch.

23

But the crowd had spilled onto it too. Like the game was over and everyone was too excited. But they weren't running around and chucking toilet rolls at each other—she'd seen the pictures on the news—but rather, they seemed to be in some sort of huge ... massive ... orgy. The camera was far enough away that you could see what they were doing, just not too many details.

Donnie dropped the glass he was cleaning. It shattered on the floor.

And Janie slipped back onto the stool.

What struck Janie was that most of the people on the pitch were men. Obviously it was expected that most of the crowd at a football match would be men, but Janie thought it odd that they were all fine with fucking each other. It was her experience that most men that went to the football were blokey-blokes who, gay or not, wouldn't admit it, not least at the game. Bunch of useless homophobes. In her experience.

Anyway, there was probably a hundred or more people in the shot, and they were all fucking. All of them. Some of them paired off, and going at it—she would use the term, normally, except, national television, football pitch—and others seemed to be in some human centipede setup with as much pleasuring going on as possible.

"Well, strike a light," Janie said. "Won't you look at that? Free love."

"Why are they all having sex?" Donnie asked.

"I don't know." Janie grinned. "But I have a new found love of the game." She tapped on the bar. "I'll have another."

"Look." Diane pointed at the screen. "There." She'd Where's Wally'd the screen and found in the bottom corner, some guy lying on the pitch. It looked like their head had been crushed, trampled. And someone was still fucking them in the arse.

"That dude *is* fucking a corpse, right?"

Then the screen went blank.

CHAPTER 5

"Someone needs to call the BBC. Make a complaint." Diane was shaking her head, staring at the imageless TV as Donnie flicked through, channel after channel.

"Jesus Christ," Janie shot her a look. "Is that all you can think of? Haven't you seen 28 Days Later?" Diane stared blankly at her. "Day of the Dead? Zombies?" She was banging her head against a brick wall. "Clearly there is something wrong with everybody." Janie pointed at the blank screen. "They were all fucking. This is Britain. People don't fuck on football pitches. Haven't you seen the news? They *fight* over them." She stood. Defiant.

"What?" Diane looked perplexed.

"This is some sort of fucking outbreak." Janie walked over to the window. Her thighs chaffed a little. She still needed to shower. She pressed her face against the window. "Donnie, where was the match?"

"I don't know," he replied quietly. "I only put the game on for the punters."

Janie looked around the empty pub. Punters. She shook her head. "I don't see anything amiss in the street. The game was probably up London way, right?"

Donnie stared blankly at her, with Diane in his arms now. She looked upset.

"Right?" This was ridiculous. "Never mind. It's

something that's spreading. We need to be aware of that. Stay away from other people. Isolate. Don't let them bite you."

"You think there was biting as well?" Diane had broken away from Donnie and was standing next to him. "I only saw people *doing it*."

"Bodily fluids," Janie continued. "Don't share bodily fluids."

"They looked like that was exactly what they were doing."

"Aargh." Janie stamped over to the bar. "You're not listening. It's fucking Romero out there." She pointed to the doors of the pub for emphasis. It was like half of her life watching horror movies in the dark was leading to this point. She sighed and looked at the non-reactions from the two of them. "Maybe you should call someone, Diane. The local council, maybe? Ask them what's up. I'm going to head home. I suggest you barricade yourself in here. The pub should be safe, yeah?"

"What makes you say that?" Donnie asked.

"I saw it in a movie." She turned, pulling her skirt down a little, still aware of her lack of knickers. She went to the door and pulled it open a crack, checking around outside. "We don't know how it transmits, yeah?"

"They were having sex," said Diane.

Janie shook her head, gave a glance back. "Lock it up, eh, Donnie?" Donnie nodded. He looked unsure, like all of this was going over his head. But she couldn't worry about them. Not now. She needed to get home. Make sure Bobby was okay. She supposed. Find some knickers. Definitely find some knickers. She stepped through into the street and looked both ways. There didn't seem to be anything wrong. No flaming ambulances careening by, mowing down screaming children and colliding with cars, panicked, trying to get out of Dodge. She checked that the door was closed behind her, and hoped that they would at least consider closing up for the day. Maybe she could get some more information from the internet when she got home. She checked the road. Clear. Crossed.

Glancing in the front of the Co-op as she walked down the length of the window, she saw someone in there stacking shelves. Good. Normality. That was what she wanted. Normality and a sense that everything was going to be okay.

She reached the end of the line of shops, and once again, made the mistake of glancing down there. As soon as she did, she knew that those cocky bastards would still be down there smoking a joint and she would get another round of their idea of passes made at her. She stopped. The young guy who had spoken to her earlier was down there, still. He was on his own now. He was facing the wall of the shop. He was … writhing against it. He had his hands pressed flat against the painted brickwork, and was thrusting his pelvis against it, like he was doing some shit Elvis impersonation. She let out a rather involuntary *eep*. Then he looked over to her. He twisted his head, leaving his groin attached to the wall. Stood, statuesque for a moment. Then he turned. He stared at her, angry looking. Like he was really pissed at her, for whatever reason. His mouth was slack, open. Made him look a bit like a stroke victim. Janie let her eyes drift down his body.

His cock was sticking out of his jeans. Hard. He had been rubbing it against the wall, seeking some sort of perverted satisfaction. Unperturbed by the fact that the wall had mangled the thin skin that surrounded his thing. The foreskin was torn and hanging off, blood pumped from the end of it like cum—maybe it *was* bloody cum—and his phallus looked generally like it had been in a motorcycle accident. Apart from that, and the slack jaw thing, he looked almost normal.

Well, for someone having sex with a wall, that was.

Janie smiled. She didn't know what else to do. She averted her eyes, and turned to leave, but he started towards her. Cock out. And she immediately knew what was coming. She broke into a run. Down the path, heading out of the estate. She cursed herself. She should have run straight back to the pub, but she just ran in the direction she was going. A quick look over her shoulder, and she could see him behind. Not far. Flip-flops were not running shoes. "Fuck," she shouted. Schlip-schlap-schlip-schlap-schlip-schlap. Fucking hell. She turned again, looked over her shoulder.

Fucker was right there.

"Rape," she shouted.

She looked around the street as the two of them ran. It was about right, wasn't it? The busiest, shittiest estate in the county. Drug dealers on every corner. Ninety percent unemployment rate. And now. Right now. There wasn't a single fucking person in the street. He grabbed her, dragging her down like they were playing rugby. She hit the paving slabs hard, and fast enough to skid. The skin on the palms of her hands tore, sliding up towards her wrists, grit and gravel digging into the supple flesh below. She made a screeching sound like a velociraptor. Turned. He was clawing his way up her body. Cock between them. He was going to fucking rape her in the middle of the fucking estate, in the middle of the fucking street, in the middle of the fucking day.

Fucking, fuck, was he.

Janie pulled her bloody hands towards her face, exposing *his* face to *her* elbows and she started digging them in. As hard as she could, at anything she could. She felt bone on bone. Bone on flesh. She stabbed them at him. Screamed. She kicked out, flip-flops flying everywhere. Landed one knee in his balls. He grunted, but never spoke. He stared into her eyes. Wild. It was like he was some animal. He *was* some animal. He was trying to get her arms in his grip, stop her from hitting him. "Fuck you," she screamed in his face, rolling her throat and spitting stringy mucus into his eyes, his skin bloody from the elbowing. He made some roaring sound like he was kid, and she rolled him off to the side, parting them, if only briefly. She pushed herself up to her knees, mirrored by his actions. She grabbed out, getting a handful of privet hedge and using it to drag herself to her feet. He got up by his own steam, blood pissing out of his cock, his eyes bulging where she'd pummelled him, a split lip. Nose bleeding onto his upper lip. Into his mouth.

He had it.

He was a fucking sex zombie.

Eww.

She looked at her flip-flops on the other side of him. Oh well. Turning she threw herself in someone's front gate, into their front garden. He lunged at her, missing, giving her time to quickly decide whether or not it was worth the risk of trying to get the owners attention. They could have it too. It was already here.

Clearly.

Then he was there, right in front of her. He swung out with his right arm, a pathetic grab. Maybe the blood that was gushing over the pavement, down the side of the Co-op, and over this poor sod's front garden had something to do with that? She lost her footing staggering into a rose bush. Stupid thorns digging into her bare legs, then she was over, the grass verge. Landed heavy on the well-manicured lawn. She reached out. Grabbed the first thing she saw, and swung it around, wielding it in front of her.

A gnome.

She pushed herself up. Tears streamed down her face. "I will fuck you up," she said through shaking lips.

He came at her.

"Well fuck you, too," she said. She jabbed the concrete pointy hat of the garden gnome into his gut, pushing him backwards. He staggered back, away from her, tangling on the bushes. She took her opportunity and raised the gnome up, over her head and slammed it down on his skull. The thud was disappointingly dull, but his head gave in more than the tiny statue did. He stopped moving, and for the first time his hard-on wavered. He looked at her, the anger gone, replaced with apathetic benevolence. Maybe he was thankful? She staggered away from him, his head seeming to want to hold onto the gnome, and she let it go, falling backwards onto her rump, her skirt riding up to her waist.

He reached up and touched the concrete ornament, impaled into his brain. His fingers felt around it as his brain matter slooped out of the side of the hole, and down, onto his jaw line. Viscous clear liquid was joining it, and a fair amount of blood. The geyser in his trouser region was lessening though, and it looked like he might stop. He dropped, arse first into a rose bush on the other side of the path, when the front door of the house opened and an elderly gentleman in a beige cardy stood there. He looked at the mushed up man in his rose bush whose brains were everywhere, and then to Janie, whose vagina was displayed directly at him.

He shook his head. "What's the world coming to?" he said, and turned back into the house, closing the door.

Janie got up and pulled her skirt down. "The fuckers can be killed," she said. "Thank fuck for that." She looked at the house. The man and—presumably—his wife were standing in the bay window looking at her. The wife had a phone in her hand and was dialling. Janie looked over to the man in the rose bush. The man she'd, by all accounts, just murdered. Until this was all out in the open, perhaps she should make haste, she thought.

C H A P T E R   6

Janie hurried out of the gate and onto the path. She looked back towards the pub and then thought better of it. They would have locked up by now. Hopefully have enough smarts to not answer to the door to anyone. *Hopefully*. Best she headed back to the flat anyway. She should be able to guarantee safety there.

Well, from the outside world, anyway.

She picked up her flip-flops and pulled them back on. The scarring on her hands stung, and the blood that dribbled from them, letting up a little. The scratches from the rose bushes on her legs itched like cat scratches. She half ran along the path as much as her footwear would allow. A car drove by. Normally. She slowed.

Her mind was awash with thoughts. The most prominent was that perhaps she had imagined all this, and possibly just murdered someone who wasn't being controlled by some sex brain virus, thing. But, if that were the case, she reasoned, then he was a rapist motherfucker and deserved everything he got. But she did feel a little sorry for the elderly couple who had a mashed up dead body in their front garden.

She could hear sirens on the air.

Coming from the main road.

Janie ducked into one of the many alleyways that criss-crossed the estate. Rabbit warren it was. For dealers, and whores. Although where the money came from, God only knew.

Crime, perhaps?

Janie waited as the sirens got louder. She couched down and kept a careful watch around the corner. If they were coming to the house she'd just left, they'd surely be looking for her too. She could just see it now. *Yes*, the old woman was saying down the phone. *A half naked tart murdered some poor boy in our front garden. What was she wearing? Not enough, I'd say.*

"Oi." A woman's voice from behind her, in the alley. Janie spun around. It was Lillian. Lillian—Lil, for short—was from the other side of the estate. She was in school with Janie a few years back, a year below her, but had gotten kicked out. She'd been expelled for playing with the boys at lunch time.

"Heya," Janie answered, turning back to look down the road again. To be honest, the two of them hadn't spoken much in the last twelve months. Before that, they had been known to drink together. But only out of convenience, not really friendship. Lil came up to her side and joined her, bent down and looked around the corner.

"Whatadoin?" she asked, a whisper.

"Did you see the football?" Janie asked without looking away from the road. She could almost see the traffic lights on the main road from there.

"The football? Did I fuck. Daryl wanted to put it on so I went over to Wesley's to get some smoke."

35

Janie glanced at her. "You're still with Daryl?"

"Of course. Massive boy he is. Love it."

"Huh." Janie continued to look up the road. "'Kay."

"What's that about the footie, anyway?"

"Oh, shit. Yeah." She stepped back away from the end of the alley and told Lil about the P.M., the football match fuckfest, and Rapey-McRapeface. All the while Lil stood there with her mouth slightly open, frowning.

Eventually she said, "Sounds like fun."

Janie shook her head. "I don't know how it's spreading." She turned and checked out of the alley towards the road again.

"You sure you ain't been slipped some E? You sound like you're tripping."

"Fuck off," she replied. "I'm heading back to my place. There was a bad accident out front when I left. Should be clear by now. You'll be safe there."

"I should head back to Daryl." Her voice was quiet. "You know, I've never known you to be wrong before."

Janie had been wrong before. Many, many times. Many. *Like that time she met a bloke called Bobby and ended up sleeping with him and moving in together somehow.* But Lil was a trusting sort.

"I'm coming with you," Lil suddenly declared.

"Good." Janie watched the police car pass the

traffic lights and stay on the main road. It wasn't coming for her. Thank fuck.

"You hiding from the pigs?"

"Yeah. Murdered some dude, remember?"

"Oh, yeah." The years and years of drug abuse had weighed heavily on Lil's short term memory and ability to focus. "Come on then. Where you at, remind me."

Janie followed her out into the street and overtook her on the path. "Come on," she said. "On the main road."

———

The car that had smacked into the man earlier outside her flat had been dragged to the side of the road to allow one side of it to be reopened. Janie looked at the dark bloodstain on the road where it used to be. There were police everywhere. One of them put his hand up and stopped Janie as she tried to pass him to get to the flat. "Sorry, Miss," he said. "You'll need to cross to the other side. There's been an accident."

No shit.

"I live here," she said, pointing to the front door of the flat.

"Did you see the accident?" he asked.

She shook her head. Didn't want to get involved. Besides, there were too many people about. However this thing travelled, it hit the match hard and fast. She just wanted to be inside. The policeman nodded, and lifted the tape for her to go into the front gate of the building. She stopped, Lil bumping into the back of her, as she left the path, turning back to him. "What happened?" she asked. "Was anyone hurt?"

"It was quite bad, miss," he replied. That was all she was getting.

Fatality then.

C H A P T E R   7

Lil slumped down on the sofa, Bobby was on the Playstation, sitting on the floor between the sofa and the TV. No fucking surprise there. "Where have you been?" he said. Didn't take his eyes from the screen. Wanted to show some dominance, but didn't actually care. Obviously.

"Did you see the accident outside?" Janie asked. She dropped down the flap on the drinks cabinet that they'd picked up from a charity shop a couple of months ago. At least he hadn't touched the vodka that was in there. He didn't answer her question, so he either wasn't listening—which was most likely—or hadn't seen the accident. Either way, what did she really care? She poured herself and Lil a shot glass of the liquid and went and sat next to her on the sofa. Lil was watching the TV with some intensity. The last few times that Janie had spent any real time with her, Lil had seemed to have trouble focusing on anything for more than a few minutes. It was like her attention span was shot to shit. Video games seemed to have the quick fire action that she needed to keep her eyes on it. Janie looked at the screen. Some sort of driving game. With guns.

At least Bobby was wearing some clothes now. He had pulled on a vest and pair of cargo shorts. She sipped her drink. And glanced to Lil. She was enthralled. Hence the three of them sitting in silence. "Fucking hell," she muttered. No point in asking to see the news or try the TV channels then.

She pulled her phone out from between the cushions and unlocked it. The battery only had fifty percent left on it. "You been using my phone?" she asked, pushing her toes into the small of Bobby's back to hopefully get his attention. He just grunted. He was holding the controller like a steering wheel and leaning to the sides when he went around corners like he was in a real car. She could see him even trying to see over hills. Stupid fuck.

Something on his shoulders caught her attention. She leaned forward, putting the phone down next to her. "What's this?" She reached towards him, but didn't touch, like it might burn her.

"What?" he asked. Aggravated.

She didn't bother responding. Fuck him if he was going to be like that. But she got a little closer. It was a rash of some sort. It was red. Really red. Like a fucking burn mark. Raised. It looked like it was getting pus-y under the skin. She looked at Lil, her attention still on the TV. *What if Bobby had it?* Shit. What should she do? She picked her phone back up and went over to the drinks cabinet. Poured herself another. She stood facing the cabinet, her drink and the phone on the flap. She flipped the phone to the internet. Google News.

Fuck.

The top stories. All of them. Panic in the streets. People are dying. What the fuck was going on? She opened one of the stories. It was garbled mess. Like the reporter had typed all this shit in a phone while trying to run or drive or something. People. Voracious acts of carnality. Fucking hell. Why couldn't they just say sex?

Janie skimmed down the article looking for symptoms. Nothing. It was just rambling panic. She went back to the results page, tried another. Much the same. It was … was… chaos.

She looked back over to Bobby. He'd put the controller down on the floor. Still staring at the TV. She shot a look to Lil. Still watching. There was nothing happening on the screen. What was she looking at? "Lil," she said.

Lil turned her head slowly. She looked straight at Janie. She smiled a little. Still held her glass of vodka, untouched.

"What's wrong?" Janie asked.

Lil looked at the back of Bobby's head. Then she reached forward and touched him. On the shoulders. On that rash. Urg. She leaned forward and put her glass on the carpet. A second hand went onto Bobby, one on each shoulder. She was rubbing him. Massaging him. He was responding. Head back. Eyes closed. Fuckers. "I am still here you know." She'd always suspected that Bobby would fuck around on her should he feel like it, but she didn't expect him to be so … brazen.

Janie watched, frozen to the spot. Vodka in one hand, phone in the other. Bobby turned, pulling away from Lil's grip, Lil's fingers, her palms, pulling the skin back on his shoulders, parting the bumping calloused rash-skin from the flesh, pus oozing onto her hands. She didn't even flinch. Janie swigged the glass of vodka. She realised it was happening. Right here. The two of them.

Bobby got to his knees, facing Lil. He pulled the zip open on his shorts. Janie could see before he did, that he was already hard. Twice in one day. Fuck. There *was* something wrong with him.

He got his cock out and started stroking it. Wanking himself off, staring at Lil. It was like he didn't even know Janie was still in the room. Lil stood up. She pulled her t-shirt up over her head. Janie could see her back. The rash. Just like the one on Bobby's shoulders. It was swamping her flesh, over her shoulders, under her bra straps. Yellow pustules were growing and throbbing like it was alive.

Janie pulled back, banging herself on the drinks cabinet.

Lil reached forward, taking his cock in her hands. Janie could see then, the rash he had. It was there too. It must have been covering his body. Blotched. Gross. He was staring into Lil's eyes. Licked his lips. He pushed forward onto her, and the two of them dropped to the sofa. He was thrusting his groin back and forth, fucking her hands, before she let go and pushed her left hand into her trackie bottoms. Under the elastic. She started frigging herself below the thin material. Bobby reached down to her bra, pulling at it, loosening it enough and then man-handling it from her torso.

The rash was over her tits.

He pushed his hands onto them. Squishing them and squeezing them like she might enjoy it. All the while she yanked him with one hand, fingering herself with the other. He grunted somewhere between satisfaction and frustration, dragging himself off her, and standing. He pulled her bottoms off, revealing the rash on her legs, her hand down the front of her knickers. His eyes brightened. He pushed his shorts off, his boxers. Got down onto his knees, and grabbed her hand, moving it away from her cunt. He pushed her knickers to the side and stuck his cock in her. Hard.

It was the most rapey, disgusting thing she had ever witnessed, yet Lil didn't seem to mind. She had wrapped her legs around him, pulling him closer.

Janie blinked. Part of her wanted to scream at the two of them. Disgusting fucking shitbags for fucking there. Right there. In front of her.

The other part of her wanted to throw up.

Instead, she made a vague motion in the direction of the door and hurried out, all the while neither of them were paying her any attention. She went to the bathroom and looked in the mirror.

Frantic.

Janie pulled at her clothes, looked under her skirt, around her slit, where he'd touched her earlier, the sides of her legs. She pulled her shirt off, her bra, pulled her breasts up and looked underneath them in the mirror. Turned around, arching to see her back.

She couldn't see any sign of the rash.

Thank fuck.

There was a shout, and a scream from the living room. Could have been them getting off together. Whatever the fuck it was, she wasn't about to hang around to find out. The flat certainly wasn't the safest place to be. She started to dress again, keeping one foot at the base of the bathroom door to hold it closed, in case either of them came looking for her. Bobby might want seconds.

She put her bra and shirt back on, quickly bandaged her palms, and then hurried back to the bedroom. Pulled a pair of knickers on, up, under her skirt. A pair of trainers. There was more noise from the living room. She crossed to the kitchen and got a knife from the drawer. They only had stupid little, shitty knives. Fuck it. It was better than nothing. She picked up her handbag from the kitchen table and slipped her phone into it. Went out into the hallway.

She could still hear them fucking.

The rash had obviously improved Bobby's performance. She couldn't help but raise a small smile. At least, the relationship was over. But she did feel for Lil. Although what would have happened if Bobby hadn't been there, she didn't know. Looking from the front door to the living room door, Janie looked into the living room. Through the crack between the door and the frame where the hinges were. Morbid curiosity. Lil was kneeling on the sofa, naked, her arms draped across the back of it, and Bobby was behind her, ploughing her from behind.

Naked too. The rash was covering both of them almost completely. Red raw skin on every inch of them. It had spread since she had left the room only minutes before. Like the act itself, the fucking, was increasing it virulence. Helping it spread.

Bobby yelled out as he came. But he didn't stop. He just kept banging back and forth. Janie looked down between them. There was cum already. He'd blown his load at least once in the last few minutes, and then again, just now. Lil was making a constant grunt, with each push. And Janie could see the rawness of the skin when they touched. Bobby was rubbing his hands over her, over her back and her tits, grabbing, clawing at them. The skin where the rash was red, burning. Scrapes and scars in the flesh appearing. Bleeding. Dripping with raw pus as they ground together.

"Fucking hell," she whispered.

Janie left the spot behind the door … and the flat. Out the front to the street. There were still people. She saw a car flash through the traffic lights. There was a person down the street, they looked confused. It could have been the rash. They could have had whatever it was. She looked around. The police had gone from the scene of the accident. But not just gone. It looked like they'd fled.

Janie looked down the street. She needed to go. Get out of the open. Fuck knows what was going on. The pub. It was the best place. It was close. She pulled her phone out of her bag as she hurried along the path.

Dialled her mum.

"Come on," she said. It rang and rang. No answer. Didn't go to voice mail either. "Fucking hell." She turned down into the estate. Kept a lookout as she walked. Down the alleyways, behind her. She looked into people windows as she passed. Sometimes she saw people in their houses. Some of them were doing normal things like they hadn't heard yet. Like they hadn't seen what was going on. Hopefully the pub would be like that.

She crossed the street when she got to the house where she had gnomed that dude to death in the front garden. It was probably best not to get too close in case the old couple were still there. The police maybe. But there were no cars. From the other side of the road she could see the body in the rose bush still. Limp. Blood pooled at his feet.

At least the motherfucker was flaccid now.

What with all his blood being elsewhere.

She could see the old couple in the window. He was banging her. The old woman was perched in the bay, and he was jack hammering against her. Huh.

Janie kept moving. This was all too terrifying and weird for her to observe the strange. She dialled nine-nine-nine and the line came up busy. How the fuck was that busy? As she got up to towards the shops she thought about going in. Maybe getting some supplies to take over the pub.

But surely they'd have anything she needed.

They'd look after her, right?

There was a scream in the distance. Janie looked around. She saw a young man run across the street behind her. He'd come from the alley that she'd bumped into Lil in, before. He sprinted out, into the street, and across, into the alley as it continued on the other side of the road. As he disappeared from sight, another man appeared from the alley. Chasing him.

It was rampant.

A fucking apocalypse.

Literally.

Shit. Janie hurried across the street to the pub. She tried the door. Open. "Fucking hell," she blurted. She pushed the door in and swung around, shutting it behind her, and slamming the bolt at the top across. "I told you to lock up," she said. She turned back into the bar.

Donnie was on the floor. Half visible from behind the bar.

She could see the top half of him. He was bleeding. Blood caked his forehead. His eyes were shut. He was moving, though. He looked like he might be having a fit of some sort, his body rocking back and forth. "Donnie?" she wanted his attention, to see if he was awake, but the words came out muted. She ran over to him, dropping down on her knees next to him. "Donnie," she said again, reaching out this time.

There was a noise from behind the bar. Enough to make her jump, her heart missed a beat. Fuck. She scooted back away from the bar. She should have checked behind it. Stupid. Janie got to her feet again, quietly. She listened. There was more noise. Rustling. Scraping. She reached over and picked up an empty glass from the bar. Instinctively she sniffed it. Stout. It was probably hers from earlier.

What was she doing? She held it at the bottom, out in front of her like a dagger. *Then* she remembered she'd picked up a knife from the flat. Oh well. She had this now. Janie edged around the bar, side stepping to keep herself facing whatever was around there.

She looked, a quick glance to see before committing, and leaping out to face … a young man. Maybe in his teens. He was hunched over Donnie. Donnie was face down on the floor, his shirt pulled up at the base of his back, and there was blood. Lots of blood. Glass everywhere. The guy had a long shard of broken pint glass in his fist and was digging at Donnie's back. Near the kidney area. The blood was spewing from the wound he'd created. A hole. Trench. It filled with blood and trickled over the side. Janie stared in horror at the man. He was grinning maniacally. The rash was all up in his face. His eyes met hers, and she wielded the glass at him, trying to be threatening when all she wanted to do was throw up.

The man discarded the glass and looked at his handy work. He made a strange chirping noise, somewhere between a cat and a sparrow. Then he leaned himself up, onto his knees, and dropped his trousers. He was commando.

He was hard.

He positioned himself quickly over Donnie and jammed his dick in the wound he'd created on his back.

Janie retched. She made an unavoidable donkey noise, drawing the man's look to her. He was thrusting in and out of the wound now. Two strokes to rhythm. Each time he pushed in, Donnie's body squirted out more of his blood like a water pistol, up the man's front wetting him, slooging Donnie's liquid up and over his t-shirt. "Jesus fucking Christ," she blurted. He didn't stop with his motion. Like the rolling of the sea, but faster. Desperate. Like he was on the clock. Under a timer. He was grinning at Janie. Drool leaving his lips and running down his chin like a head case.

Janie looked at the glass in her hand and then to this monster. This sex zombie. "Aargh," she shouted, lunging forward with the glass, swing it at the side of the infected's head.

CHAPTER 9

The glass donked off the side of his—its—head, not breaking. Janie was, in all fairness, a little disappointed. The man wavered a little, surprised, perhaps, but didn't stop fucking Donnie's body. Janie looked at him, glanced to the glass, and then back to him. Then she smacked the rim of the glass on the side of the bar, smashing it into a jagged toothy affair of very jabby things. "Ha," she shouted, and then tried hitting at him again.

This time she slashed the broken glass across his face, the side of his head, part of his ear lobe detached and went flying across the bar, plopping onto one of the bar stools. He just grinned, blood seeping at first from the cat scratch wounds on his head. Then they started to pour, blood weeping on the rash.

But none of this stopped him.

Janie got up, stood over him, raised the glass up. He looked up at her, still rolling his hips as his cock slid about in Donnie. "Stop with the fuckening," she said, slamming the glass down into the middle of this fuckers face.

The glass shattered more as it hit the bone, tearing its way through the flesh of the man's face. It de-gloved a large portion of his head, leaving the white of the bone of his skull, glistening under some mixture of liquids, blood and weeping fluids, clear, mixing together to some pink foul smelling, gross, soup. She could still see his smile under the flap of skin that hung down. One of his eyes was gone.

Janie raised her foot and planted it flat on the fuckers chest, hard, kicking him from his precarious position, down, onto his back beyond Donnie. "Fuck you," she said. She glanced down at Donnie. Now, without this monster fucking a hole in his back, Donnie wasn't moving at all. Janie leapt over him, down onto the zombie-thing, onto her knees over its belly. She brought the broken glass up. Down. Up. Down. Stabbing indiscriminately into the creatures face, its neck. Chest. Shoulders. With each blow, more of the things flesh parted from his head, its torso. Bits of it flew up into the air, followed by sprays of blood like some twisted shampoo commercial. She stabbed down onto its shoulder as it tried to struggle against her, cutting through its flesh, muscles, hacking at the ligaments of the left arm. Eventually it stopped moving. The arm. The things face was a mush of flesh and bone, she could see its nose bone. Teeth loose and out, blood running from its mouth. It was still flopping about beneath her.

Not dead.

Why wasn't it dead yet?

Then she could feel it moving its right arm. It was trying to get it around, underneath her arse, trapped below her. Doing … something. She lifted the glass back up, strewn with gore, flesh stuck to it. It looked like one of those things in the window of a kebab shop. Like an elephants leg of raw meat.

He was still moving his arm, but wasn't trying to

escape. It wasn't trying to fight her off. It was …

"Oh," she screamed, pulling herself off the things stomach and onto her feet. She didn't want to look, but couldn't stop herself. He—it—had wrapped its fingers around its still hard cock and was stroking itself. Stunned, she looked up its body. The further her eyes travelled up it, the more of a mess it became, until the face, barely recognisable as human. Its blood had leeched over the floor, a pool of ever extending blood circling outwards.

Its hand was getting slower, as the bubbles that plopped through the blood that filled where its mouth used to be, stopped.

Its hand relaxed.

Its cock waned as blood stopped pumping around its body.

"Fucking hell," she whispered. Janie looked down at herself. She was painted in the creatures innards. Blood. Bits of its face. Tongue. Plasma. Fuck. Her attention fell to Donnie. "Shit," she muttered, dropping down next to him, releasing the glass from her hand. "Don," she said. He hated it when anyone called him that. "*Don*," she said again. She pushed him, trying to roll him over. There was a lot of blood over him and the floor. She felt his neck looking for a pulse. She didn't find one, but didn't really know if she was putting her fingers in the right place, either.

Janie tenderly ran her fingers over the area of his head that was bleeding. It was dented. Like it shouldn't have been. Poor fuck was probably dead before he hit the ground. She looked at the wound in his back. Maybe it was just as well.

She got to her feet and pulled the kitchen knife out of her bag. "Diane?" she called. "Diane, can you hear me?" She went through to the back of the pub, holding the knife out in front of her, like she might be jumped at any second. "You here? It's me, Janie."

CHAPTER 10

"Diane," she called. "Are you there?" Janie held the knife out and pushed the door behind the bar open. Beyond was darkness. There were no windows. She looked around. There was a strip of light under the door to the left. A stairwell in front. The stairs must go to the flat upstairs. She'd seen the windows from out the front, and had always assumed that the two of them must live up there. She knocked on the door on the left, knife still held in the other hand. "Diane?"

"Who's there?" Diane's voice came from the other side of the door. It was quiet. Weak.

"It's me," Janie said. "Janie. Can I come in?" She heard the bolt on the other side of the door slide across. Janie turned the handle and opened the door just a crack. "You okay?" she asked.

"Where's Donnie?" Diane replied. "He made me come in here and promise not to open up unless it was him."

Janie looked down at herself. This wasn't going to be easy. She opened the door a little further, but didn't step in. "He's in the bar," she said quietly. "I think he's ..." Her voice drifted to silence as Diane started to wail. Janie pushed the door open, wanting to comfort her, and Diane looked up. She froze in mid-cryface, and Janie realised what she must look like. "Fuck," she said quietly. "It's not what you think."

Well it wasn't, technically.

Diane was sitting on the edge of the bath. The room on the left was a small, yet fully furnished bathroom for use by the staff. Why they had a bath in it, Janie didn't know. Diane screamed out in sadness and Janie hurried over, sitting beside her, pushing the bloodless knife into her bag. "Someone had come into the bar," she said. She put her arm around Diane's shoulders and got blood and shit all over her. "I fucked him up good and proper though." Diane was nod-crying. At least she seemed to understand.

"You've got blood on you," she said.

Janie nodded. *No shit.* She looked into the bath behind them. There was a shower on the wall. "Any chance I could," she nodded at the shower, feeling bad for asking. But she was covering in the infected's blood, after all.

Diane nodded, getting to her feet. She waved at the door and said, "I'll just ..." she was still crying.

"Don't go in the bar," Janie warned. "Why don't you go upstairs? Make us a nice cup of tea, and I'll be up shortly."

Diane nodded and left the bathroom, turning and going upstairs. Janie went to the door and watched her. She then closed and bolted it. She pulled her clothes off her as fast as she could, turning the shower on at the same time. The water ran cold. Fucks weren't given. At least her underwear was bloodless. She dropped them in the dry sink to keep them away from the rest of the clothes, strewn about the floor and getting everything muddy-red. She stepped under the cold water, shivering hard. The icy water refreshed her, while making her shake. And once she started shaking she couldn't seem to stop.

"It's just shock," she said to herself, over and over. Looking down, the water in the bath ran from red to pink, to clear as the gore and blood, sloshed down into the tub and most of it washed away. Eventually she was left standing in ankle deep water, after the plug was blocked with bits of *it*. She got out the shower and stood in front of the mirror naked. She examined herself now she was clean, looking for signs of the rash.

Part of her felt she was being paranoid, blaming this rash for it, but the other part of her told her it wasn't just a coincidence.

She seemed to be clean. Free of it.

Thank the fucking Lord.

She pulled her underwear back on and looked at her skirt and shirt. Both fucked up with the blood of a monster. Blood she had no particular desire to get close to, let alone dress in. She took her bag, grabbing the knife again and holding it out, before opening the bathroom and looking out into the corridor beyond. Still in her underwear. She looked around—couldn't see much without the light—and then slipped out into the corridor and onto the stairs. She padded, nearly naked up to the flat upstairs, barefoot, but armed. Wet, but clean.

Janie got to the door at the top of the stairs. A

front door like you would have in the street. Good. At least it should be secure. She knocked. "Diane, it's me," she hissed, still trying to be as quiet as she could.

Diane opened the door like nothing was wrong. She looked down Janie, and said, "Oh, look at you." She turned and shambled down the hallway and off to the side. She was wearing a pair of carpet slippers. She wasn't before. She was wearing shoes. Fuck it. She'd lost it. Janie entered the flat. It was warm. The carpet was welcoming on her bare feet. She closed the door behind her and made sure it was secure.

Diane reappeared with a small pile of clothing. "Here," she said. "This might fit."

Janie didn't give two shits if it did or didn't, really. Clothes were clothes. She pulled a t-shirt over her head, and dragged on a pair of jeans. The jeans were a little too long, but about right around the waist. Diane's. The t-shirt was massive. Donnie's. She shivered and hugged herself.

"Tea?" Diane said, wandering to the end of the hallway and into the kitchen.

Janie nodded, following her, behind. This wasn't going to be easy.

C H A P T E R   1 1

Janie followed Diane into the kitchen. She was smiling. Humming the tune of some soap opera. What the fuck. She'd lost her marbles, clearly. Christ. Janie slipped down into an empty seat at the kitchen table and watched the woman potter around.

Making tea.

"You okay?" she asked as she watched.

"Uh, huh." An agreement. Vague, but sure.

"He didn't suffer," Janie offered. It didn't seem like much, and Diane stopped. She had just put the teabags in the pot. Very old fashioned. She hung her head. Just a little. Like she was thinking. "What can I do?" Janie asked.

"Fuck me," she said.

Shit.

"What?" Janie asked, quietly. She put her hand in her bag and gripped the knife again, waiting for sex-zombie Diane to turn and pounce.

"I said, fuck me," she replied. "Excuse the language."

Janie let her grip loosen a little. "You okay?" she asked again, this time more tentatively.

Diane nodded without turning. "I just thought that Donnie and me, well, we were going to make it, you know? I was married before." She continued to make the tea. "Violent bastard he was. Used to knock me about a bit. Got all fighty when his dinner wasn't on the table in time." Janie could hear her crying gently as she spoke. "One day Donnie came round. He knew my ex from work. We'd never met. And my ex just slapped me for not plating up for another. Of course, I didn't know that Donnie was coming over, did I? How could I. Should have used that sixth sense. The one that would stop me from getting the shit kicked out of me for no reason.

"Donnie watched him do it. I've never had someone defend me before. But Donnie wasn't having none of it. He stood up to my ex like I'd never seen anyone do before. He got between us. Told Peter—my ex—that he needed to back away. That he couldn't hit a woman. It was very gallant. My knight in shining armour."

Diane put a cup of tea down on the table in front of Janie, and sat opposite, with one of her own.

"Peter raised his hand up to hit Donnie. And Donnie wasn't going to have any of that, either. He pushed him aside and grabbed the cleaver that I had been cutting the beef up with for the curry. I was making curry. Peter liked that. Anyway, he hit Peter in the neck with it. It was like he was some angel of death, there to protect me from evil. Killed Peter instantly." Diane looked Janie in the eyes for the first time and smiled. "I don't suppose it matters me telling anyone now. Does it?"

Janie shook her head, speechless.

"The end of the world, and all. So after Donnie

59

had pulled the cleaver out of his neck, Peter fell to the floor. I couldn't help myself. I tore that man's clothes off like a horny groupie, and I had him, right there in the kitchen, next to my ex's body. Best. Sex. Ever. Then we loaded the body up in the boot of Donnie's motor and drove it down to the Black Forest. Buried him. I told everyone that cared—not a lot of people did—that he'd run off with some tart and no one thought enough of him to disagree, and I moved away with Donnie." She looked around the room. "We brought this place and lived happily ever after." She sighed. "Well, until now."

Janie realised her mouth was open slightly so she pulled it together. "Well," she said. She had always thought that the two of them were just married. Childhood sweethearts, or something. Nothing so grand in their history as a murder-rescue-thing. It was quite sweet actually. Janie wondered if she'd have thought as much if she hadn't murdered one or two people this morning herself. "So what are we going to do?"

Diane looked up at her. "Oh, yes. I'll put the radio on. You see if there's anything on the Internet. You should pick up the free wi-fi from the bar up here." She got up and went over to the radio, acting like none of this was happening. Like her ... husband? ... wasn't lying in a pool of blood in the bar downstairs.

She was concerned about Diane's mental health, but still did what she had suggested.

Janie pulled her phone from her bag and opened

Google news again. The stories were mounting. None of them used the *Z* word. No one had thought to call them sex zombies, not yet, but the reports were there. There was panic on the streets. People were turning on each other. The reports kept using the word assault. Stay in your homes they were saying. She scrolled from site to site. There were people putting up video footage. People fucking in the street. Some of them weren't infected. Being raped. Others were. They were just fucking each other raw. Some weren't moving. Like Donnie. Janie shook her head and closed the browser. She turned to Diane. She was going from channel to channel.

"Most of the big stations aren't there, or are just playing music. Probably their emergency no-one-turned-into-work playlist. Here, this is Birchingate FM. It broadcasts from the school around the corner."

The national news outlets are telling people to stay in their homes. I've seen what's happened even at the station here, and I don't know if that's going to make a difference. I'm locked inside my booth and I'm staying here. I'll transmit as long as I can. Trying to make anything out of the conflicting reports from across the UK, it doesn't look localised, but it doesn't look like it's happening anywhere else in the world either. Some people are blaming science. Others are saying it's retribution from God. Either way, it doesn't look good.

Diane turned the radio off and stared at it. "Now what?"

"We barricade ourselves in and hope for the best,

I suppose."

CHAPTER 12

"You don't need to do this." Janie was standing between Diane and the door to the bar.

"We need to make sure that they're dead. And you're the one who keeps mentioning zombies. We need to make sure that they aren't going to rise from the grave and eat our brains."

"It's not a movie," Janie said. She realised how weak the argument was before she'd finished saying it. Zombies, no, of course not. Sex-zombies? Well, that was a different matter. She nodded. "Yeah, okay." She pushed the door open and stuck her head around into the bar. There were no zombies, sex or otherwise. The two of them had been upstairs for a couple of hours and the smell in the bar was awful. Sure, it was a warm summery day, but Janie hadn't expected them to turn bad quite that quickly. She stepped out and held her hand over her mouth. Donnie was laying on the floor, unmoved. He didn't look any different than when she had left him. Maybe the pooled blood was blacker. His skin paler. As she walked around the bar, the stench got stronger. She looked at the man she'd killed. The zombie. Excuse me, sex-zombie. He was mashed up, just as she had left him, but he was rotting. Fast. It was like he'd been dead for days. Maybe longer. Even through her hand, Janie could smell him. No, she didn't know what dead bodies should smell like, but this wasn't right.

"What the fuck is that?" asked Diane.

Janie shook her head. The corpse's blood had dried out, turned black, and started to flake away like paint spilled yesterday. His flesh was hard like beef-jerky. He smelt like three-day-old turkey that hadn't been refrigerated. She knelt down next to it. "It's not right," she said. "I ain't no doctor, but decomposition like this shouldn't happen in the span of hours, right?" She could see maggots in the wounds. Glancing to Donnie and back, Donnie was still … juicy. That was probably the wrong word. This one? He'd dried out. A husk. She'd seen Criminal Minds. This was the body of someone dead for a week or more. "This might be important." Janie turned back to Diane.

She was standing over Donnie, staring at the wounds on his back, on his head. Tears on her cheeks.

Janie got up and pulled Diane's face into her shoulder. "Come on," she whispered. "Let's get you out of here." She led the woman back out to the hallway and the stairs. "Why don't you go upstairs and have a lie down? I'll grab some table cloths." Diane nodded and turned up the stairs. Janie went straight back into the bar. She held her hand over her mouth. The stank made her want to throw up. Her stomach rolled over and over, until it made her want to shit too. She went from window to window making sure everything was secured. She checked the door she'd locked earlier. Then out to the kitchen. Back door to the fire escape. More windows. She made sure that *everything* was locked up before she rummaged around in the backroom to find something to cover the bodies.

By the time she had found a couple of dark blue table cloths—the one's they used for the occasional wedding reception—she returned to the bar to find the other corpse decomposed further. It was like time was passing differently for it. The flesh had withdrawn from its fingers making it look like its nails were still growing. She could see its teeth and gums where it had died with a maniacal grin on its face, and where she'd hacked off large chunks of flesh. Again there was decomposition.

Donnie looked like he could still turn over and get up. Brush it off like he was asleep the whole time.

What the actual fuck?

She covered the two bodies and went back upstairs. Diane wasn't in the kitchen, so Janie assumed she was in bed. Blacked out from all the stress, probably. She went to the window in the kitchen. It looked out into the street at the front of the pub. She could see the shops from there. The road. Paths. Some of the houses.

She stayed back so that anyone outside stood less chance of seeing her.

There were a few of them out there. They seemed uncontrollable. They certainly didn't try to control themselves. There were two women. They were naked. One of them was straddled across a guy laying on the path. He was screaming. Not infected. She was fucking him. The other was trying to force herself onto his mouth. All the while the two of them were playing with each other's tits. There was a man and woman fucking on a car. Apart from the man on the path, Janie could see the rash. It was swarming them. All over them.

She looked at the man. She wanted to help. Another of the infected ran by. Naked. Hard. The flesh flaying from his feet as the gravel from the road dug into it, grating the skin off. Blood trails remained where his feet had padded. He had bits of him broken, damaged. He looked like he might have been hit by a car and slid down the road. Naked. The rash was on him. Over him.

And he looked like he was falling to pieces.

Rotting away.

She pulled back from the window, unable to watch anymore. She didn't want to hear the screams of the man who wasn't infected. Well, even without knowing how the thing transmitted, he was probably infected now.

They probably all were.

Janie roamed the kitchen for a few minutes, and then sat at the table. She twiddled with her teacup, before getting up and looking to see if there was a bathroom up here, too.

CHAPTER 13

Standing in front of the mirror, Janie examined herself. Did the rash come first, before the madness? She didn't know. She'd only guessed. That was what she had seen with Bobby. Lil. She looked in her eyes first, examining how tired she looked. Then she started to pull up her clothes, checking her belly. Her breasts. She pulled her shirt off and turned, looking at her back as best she could.

She was exhausted, and hurt.

But she didn't have any signs of the infection.

Pulling her clothes back on, she went into the hallway. Had to find Diane in one of these other rooms. She was probably sleeping it off. It must have been hard to know Donnie was like that. It wasn't like that with Bobby. He was probably dead by now. She didn't want to think about it, and to be honest, didn't care much either. Listening at the first closed door on the landing, she could hear noises from beyond.

Diane.

Janie tapped her fingertips lightly on the door. She didn't know whether she should wake her or not. Maybe just push the door open and make sure she looked all right. Janie twisted the handle and opened the door a crack. A bedroom. It was dark inside. The curtains drawn. Janie could see Diane on the bed. She was under the covers. Tossing. Turning. Unsure if she was asleep, or just upset, Janie pushed the door open a little further. "Hey," she said. "You okay?"

The shuffling under the covers stopped, but she didn't reply.

The last thing Janie needed right now was for Diane to fucking turn too. Shit. She pushed the door open all the way, the light from the flat illuminating a small amount of the room. Janie stepped in. The room smelt of sweat. Dirty. Maybe it always smelt like that. Fuck it. Until a few hours ago, Donnie and Diane were the landlords of her local and passing friends at best. She'd never been up here. Maybe they were pigs in their private life?

She stepped over to the bed. Diane was covered by the sheets. Janie reached down slowly, taking the cotton in her hand and gripping it. She was going to pull it back. She thought about dragging it off her like a magician with a tablecloth and then thought better of it. If she was half asleep under there it might give her a heart attack. Janie lifted the sheet and pulled it from where her face was.

She was asleep under the covers. Likely dreaming about Donnie.

But the rash was there. On her face, just below her right eye.

"Cock," Janie whispered. She put the sheet back down. While she was asleep, that was fine, but Janie knew that she would turn. Sooner or later. She backed to the door of the bedroom, never taking her eyes from Diane, twitching in dreams. She stood there watching her. She had to leave the flat. It was the only way to guarantee some semblance of safety.

But that meant *leaving the flat.*

Fuck.

She looked at the bed. It was a pine affair. Not a bad quality. Posts at the four corners. Not like a four-poster bed or anything, but tall enough to be useful.

———

Janie had rummaged in silence around the bedroom and found a variety of ties and belts. The sort of accessories one might own if one ran a pub. She carefully tied one off at each of the posts of the bed. Then, she removed the sheet from Diane. The rash was over her face now. Up close, Janie could see how far it had spread, covering every inch of her skin above the neckline. She took Diane's wrist and lifted it carefully so as not to wake her. Over her head.

She mumbled—grumbled—in her sleep.

Then she pulled one of Donnie's ties, secured to the post, around her wrist, gently tightening it.

She did the same with the other hand.

Janie didn't want to push her luck and do the feet too. Diane could still pull herself free if she tried. The knots weren't pulled tight-tight yet. Not in case she woke her. Janie pulled the knot on Diane's left wrist tight, and then hurried around the bed, pulling the right one tight. The yank on the tie brought Diane awake, and her eyes flicked open. It took her a second of looking around to realise what had happened. Her mouth dropped open as her eyes widened. She looked at Janie. "What …" she said. "What are you doing?" She yanked on the ties trying to free herself. The knots were good though and didn't give. "What?" she pulled again, harder. *"Let me go."*

Janie drew herself back, away from her. "You've got it," she said, no more than a whisper.

"I don't. What are you saying?"

"The rash," she said. "It's all on you."

Diane's eyes looked around wildly. Her legs thrashed, kicking form side to side. Janie backed out the door and closed it. Diane was screaming. Screaming for her to free her. Let her go. *She was fine.*

Like fuck was she.

Janie rested her head against the door of the bedroom and let out a sigh, a tear running down her face. Diane was wailing. Crying too. Scared. Janie covered her ears with her palms and went over to the living room. She pushed the door closed and went, sat on the sofa. She could still hear the muffled cries coming through the thin walls.

She could still hear cries and screaming coming from outside. In the street.

Janie got up and went to the window looked out. She could just about see the street from there. The man—the one who wasn't infected. He was on his knees now. Middle of the road. Ploughing into the woman that was trying to ride his face earlier. They were bucking together like finishing was the only thing that mattered. But it wasn't. Janie had seen it now. It wasn't finishing the act. It was doing the act. She could see the other woman. The one that was fucking him before. She was lying in the street next to them. Blood everywhere. It looked from this distance like her head had been caved in, but it was hard to tell.

Not that it mattered. Some geezer was fucking the corpse anyway.

Janie suddenly felt sick. She turned and ran from the living room to the bathroom and lifted the toilet seat. She held her stomach as she heaved, leaning her head down, below waist level, allowing the free flow of vomit to come forth. The acidic puke slid from her stomach, bile and green, out through some of her hair, and into the bowl. "Fuck *in* hell," she muttered, wiping her mouth with the back of her hand. She could see stringy mucus looking sick hanging from a tuft of hair that was hanging down the side of her head. It made her want to retch again. She flushed the loo and turned to the sink, running the water, and slopping her hair under it to clean it.

Why was she barfing so often? It had been coming and going for a few days now.

Shit.

She left the bathroom. Diane's bedroom was quiet now. She went to the door and listened. Nothing. No sound of movement and no screaming.

C H A P T E R   1 4

Janie pushed the door open. Diane was on the bed. She had stopped thrashing about. Janie flicked the lights on in the middle of the ceiling. Diane was tied in a Christ pose, but she had her legs together, and was rubbing them. She looked like a spastic cricket. Janie watched her. She didn't pay Janie any attention at first. She was just focussing on this weird rubbing motion she'd gotten going. Janie though it looked like she was trying to use friction to start a fire.

Then she realised that she probably was.

She was trying to gain satisfaction by rubbing herself on the only other thing she could. Herself. Janie stepped closer to try and see how bad the rash was, and drew Diane's attention to her. She stared at Janie, the rubbing getting harder. More frantic. She started to grunt, and Janie didn't know if she was achieving her mastabatory goal, or if it was frustration. Exhaustion.

It didn't look easy. Bringing yourself off like that.

Diane's face was red, the rash raw on the skin. She'd grown pus filled boils and lesions, calluses. She looked more like a burn victim. It was like the rashes effects were moving quicker on her than other people she'd seen. Like her inability to satisfy the sexual need was connected to the rash taking hold.

Fucking hell.

Were they just fucking because of some instinctive self-preservation?

"Cunt," Janie whispered. She'd tied her up and probably quickened her death, *if* that was the case. But if she untied her, she wasn't going to be satisfied with frigging herself, now, was she?

She looked at her hands. She was shaking. Fuck. Diane's grunts were persistent. Like she was close but couldn't quite get there. Janie backed to the door. She didn't know what to do, so she drew the door closed and returned to the kitchen.

Made herself another cup of tea.

She didn't really want the tea. It was just something to do. The thought of sexually pleasing this zombie woman wasn't appealing. She picked up her phone off the kitchen table. No signal. She was utterly alone. Her eyes drifted over the things in the kitchen while she sat there, thinking. She could hear Diane in the bedroom.

Grunting. The occasional call. It was like a trapped animal desperate for freedom.

She had to do something. After all these years of Diane and Donnie being so good to her. *Shit*. Janie stood, pushing the chair back with a whining grind on the tiles of the floor. She strode into the hall and to the bedroom pushing the door back open.

Diane stopped her frustrated rubbing for a split second and looked at her. Then continued. Desperate. Janie walked in, keeping one eye on her. She went to the drawers in the cabinet by the bed and pulled the top one open on the left hand side. Pushing a couple of thrillers aside, there wasn't much in there. A wrist watch. Box of condoms. This must be Donnie's. She went around the bed, still keeping herself away from it, making sure that Diane couldn't reach her. But she was far more interested in trying to pleasure herself, zoned out in some rhythm, than anything Janie was doing.

She opened the bedside drawer on the other side. Romance novel. Horror Novel. Earrings. Mobile phone. She checked. No signal. Also, no dildo. She stood and looked at Diane. "Why did you have to have a decent sex life, eh?" She sighed. A big one. "What the fuck am I doing?" Janie left the bedroom, back to the kitchen. She pulled the fridge open. Crisper drawer. She was no good at this. It wasn't the sort of thing that Bobby would exactly approve of. If he'd caught her. She thought about him and Lil. Wondered if they'd fucked each other to death.

Janie held up a cucumber. She thought about Diane. It'd snap, surely?

"Well, fuck," she said, closing the door of the fridge. She started opening drawers in the cupboards, pulling out anything that was phallic enough. A knife. No. A whisk. Fuck no. Bottle? She stood it on the side. Not perfect but it was better than anything else at the moment. She knelt, opening a cupboard at her feet. "Ah," she exclaimed. Janie reached in and took the rolling pin. It was long, true, but that would stop her from having to get too close. It was wood, so wouldn't bend or break. These things were designed not to let splinters come off. Perfect.

She caught sight of the olive oil on the counter and went to reach for it. "Lube," she said. She stopped herself. She wasn't going to need that, was she? Not with how fucking horny these things were.

Weighing the rolling pin in her hand, she returned to the bedroom.

CHAPTER 15

"Look," she said. She was standing at the bottom of the bed holding the rolling pin. Diane was staring at her like she was a model in a dirty mag, all the while rubbing her legs together. "You need to understand that I'm just trying to help." Janie let out a little giggle at the sheer absurdity of it.

She rubbed her forehead with her hand. "What the fuck am I doing?"

She held out the pin for Diane to see. "Look," she said, again. "I'm going to ... relieve you." She held it, and Diane made no motion to suggest that she'd so much as heard her, than understood. Janie made a jabbing motion, thrusting it at her. "Like a cock," she said. "Donnie? Yes?"

Diane just kept doing what she was doing.

Janie let her hand drop to her side, and her head drop. "I've lost it," she said. "I've actually lost it." She put the rolling pin down on the set of drawers opposite the bed. Every inch of Diane was riddled with the rash now. Pus, mucus, obscure liquids ran from broken tears in her skin. Markings that looked like burns, split open and leaking. She looked like someone has taken a cheese grater to her flesh and not stopped. Parts of her were falling from the bone like she was a pot-roast. Some of her hair was loose on the sheets where it had fallen from her head.

She was beyond saving.

Janie went back to the kitchen and got a knife out the block. The one with the biggest point and went back to the bedroom. "I'm sorry, love. I just don't know how else to help you."

She came to the side of the bed. She didn't try to hide the knife, but she didn't wave it in Diane's face either. But she'd seen it. Didn't stop her from doing the leg-rubbing thing. It didn't stop her from looking at Janie like she was a stripper. "Fucking hell," Janie muttered. She raised the knife up, Diane still holding a salacious gaze.

Janie stabbed the knife down into Diane's stomach. All the way to the handle. She expected her to die, but she didn't. It didn't even seem to slow her down. She brought the knife out, and blood spurted from the hole like a geyser. Warm, and thick. "Ahh," Janie took a step back instinctively. "Fuck." She didn't want to get more of this fucking blood on her, but she'd started now. She stepped up, and stabbed down into her gut again. The only thing it achieved was more blood, and louder grunts from Diane. "Fucking hell." She pulled the knife out. Big spurt. In. Out. In. Out.

She pushed it in, twisting the blade around.

Diane was squirming. She was rubbing her legs together even harder. The grunts were turning to screams. She was hefting air in and out.

"Jesus, you're enjoying this?" Janie pulled the blade out. Bits of Diane's insides came out, wrapped around the knife. Guts. Intestines? Maybe? Janie flicked the blade and the gore and gloop slipped off, flipping around the room. Sticking to the wall like cooked spaghetti. "Oh, God." She looked at Diane.

O face.

"Fuck," she said. "No." Diane's stomach was pooled with blood, running over the edge of her flesh like a bath with the taps left on. She was screaming out in bloody ecstasy. Janie could tell she was lost in some unending orgasm. She backed away. Diane was still rubbing her legs together, trying to maintain the feelings that she was embroiled in.

Janie dropped the knife to the floor, clattering on the hardwood boards. She picked up the rolling pin and looked at it. Her face contorted in horror. Disgust. The un-naturalness of it all. "I am so sorry," she said quietly, as tears began to roll down her face. "So … sorry." She stepped up to the bed and lifted the rolling pin like a bat. She took one last look into Diane's eyes. She wasn't in there. They were just staring back. Lustful.

Horny.

Janie smacked the rolling pin down into the centre of her face, wanting nothing more than for her pain to stop. That, and the look she was giving of a horny teenage boy wanking over a copy of Big Tits Monthly. There was a cracking sound as bone gave way to wood. Janie pulled the pin back up, not wanting to look at the damage. It was hard to remove from her face, like she was holding onto it. She slammed it down again. This time she saw. She didn't mean to look. It was instinct. Diane's nose had caved in from the first blow, the bone splintering out making the middle of her face look like a meteor site. When the second blow landed it went through the skull, into the mush beneath. Diane's brain didn't splatter out and loosh all over the bedroom like Janie expected. It wasn't like the gnome incident from earlier.

Diane stopped moving. When her legs stopped, Janie was sure she'd finished moving, finally. She leaned over her. The rolling pin was stuck in her head, sticking out into the room. The smell up close was like shit blended warm with vomit. But it didn't smell like Donnie did. The smell of metal wasn't there. Janie looked at the mess inside Diane. Her brains looked like they had started some chemical reaction a while back. Solidifying.

Whatever this infection was, it was causing death pretty fucking quickly. Fucking or no fucking.

Then the smell and the sight overcame her, and Janie couldn't stop her cup of tea returning. She vomited over Diane's gaping face hole, filling the gaps with brown liquid, and weirdly, sweetcorn.

She didn't remember eating any sweetcorn recently.

CHAPTER 16

Janie sat in the chair she had pulled up to the window. She was watching the street. There were dead bodies lying in the kerb. The gutter. Once they had died, they started to decompose with haste. She found she could watch them melting away over the hours.

After she'd closed the bedroom door on Diane's corpse, she hadn't looked again. She was sure the same thing was happening to her, but she didn't want to see it. She didn't need to. She was happy to know she wasn't in pain now. Or whatever the other feeling was.

The TV was running in the corner of the room. Blue screen. Nothing was transmitting. There was the radio still running in the kitchen, but it was silent. The man on there, the one who said he would keep transmitting … he'd stopped eventually. Janie could tell by the sounds after that he'd been taken by the infection.

She hadn't though. And she didn't know why. Still hadn't and so much time had passed. There didn't even seem to be any of them left in the streets now. They were all gone. Fucked themselves to death. Or not. Depending on which way you looked at it.

Janie stood, went to the kitchen. The radio was silent. The station was still transmitting, she thought. She poked around in the washing machine and found

another clean set of clothes. A top—one of Diane's—
that should fit better than the bloody, gooey, t-shirt
she was wearing now, and a skirt. She went to the
bathroom and washed.

Cleaning Diane from her.

She checked herself in the mirror. Still no rash.
She didn't know why she'd been spared. What made
her different. She dressed and went and made some
food. Watched the street. She wasn't about to leave
the safety of the pub without knowing that this
disease had eaten them all away.

———

Two days after she'd ended Diane's suffering, Janie
decided to leave the pub. She hadn't seen another
living thing in those two days. She packed up a
carrier bag with things that she might need. A knife.
She had found a decent one. A torch. She'd dressed in
clean clothes. Managed to fashion a pair of walking
shoes that were two sizes too big to fit her using extra
socks as packing.

It had meant that she had needed to go into
Diane's bedroom. The stench coming from the room,
even before she'd opened the door, was rank. The
room was leaking this stink of rotting tinned corn
beef and vomit. She had opened the door and tried to
find everything she needed to without looking at her
on the bed.

But she had.

There was something that drew her to look. Just once.

Diane had melted away. It was like someone had poured acid over her and her skin had burned through, sliding from her bones, a rancid pool of gloop and gore wettened the bed, the floor beneath, seeping into the floorboards, down, into the pub below. And now, a couple of days later, it had jellified, leaving the look of the inside of a pork pie.

Janie had, of course, thrown up the contents of her stomach. It wasn't much—one of the reasons she was leaving now—and that had only added a battery acid flavour lingering in the mix.

She left the room with what she needed to leave the pub, vowing to never return to that room. Even if she needed to get back to the pub.

She took the keys from Donnie's dead body. The other corpse in the bar had decomposed in the same way that Diane had, but it didn't feel so bad to Janie, perhaps because she didn't know him. Either way, she prepared, and stepped out into the warm summer's day, carrier bag in one hand, kitchen knife in the other.

She half expected there to be a thousand of these sex zombies out there waiting. Hidden in the alleyways and front gardens to jump her—literally—as soon as she left the safety of the pub.

But nothing happened.

She walked quietly down the street, birds chirping like nothing was any different. Just a quiet summer's day. Closing her eyes she imagined that she could be in the middle of a field in Oxfordshire, alone, peaceful.

But all around her, the streets were littered with what remained of the corpses of the people. All of them. All except her. The people in the street had melted away, pooling into a human soup full of bones, some quicker than others. There was a body just outside the pub doors. One that she couldn't see from the window inside. It was a man. He was rotting slower than most of the bodies that she had seen from inside the pub. Very promiscuous, obviously. But the birds had been at him.

What was left of his flesh had been pecked at, and pulled. Probably the same seagulls that attacked the black sacks of rubbish people used to put out in the street the day before the bin men were due.

Except instead of banana skins and kebab wrappings strewn to the side, it was innards, intestines. Bits of some blokes insides that a seagull couldn't gobble back without choking. They really were the rats of the sky. Anyone living near the seaside could tell you that.

Janie went over to the window of the Co-op. Somehow she'd always imagined that come the end of the world, the shops would all be looted like a nineties movie. The shop was untouched apart from the one display she could see that had toppled. Possibly when the infection had hit someone in there.

She'd come back later with a backpack and stock up on food.

After being outside for a while, she was satisfied that there was no one there. No horde of mindless sex fiends waiting to rape her until she died. Or they died. Whichever happened first.

Actually, most likely, both.

She headed back towards her flat. She may as well pick up her stuff.

C H A P T E R 1 7

Janie kept her phone in her pocket the whole time. She checked it periodically. The signal would come and go, but she couldn't get a call to go through. She just got an intermittent buzzing sound out of the thing.

She stood in the door of her living room and looked at the corpses of Bobby and Lil. Well, she assumed it was them. They had melted into some blob of flesh and gristle, muscles visible, sinew hanging, frozen in the pinpoint in time where one, or the last of them had passed away.

Doing it doggy style.

She smiled. At least they both went doing what they enjoyed. The TV was still running a screen from the game that Bobby was playing. A demo-thing with a guy running around shooting everyone in the face. She took the remote from the sofa arm and flipped the channel back to one. A black screen. Something was still sending a signal, but there was no one there to say anything. She tossed the remote on the sofa next to the bodies and took the vodka bottle from the drinks cabinet, slurping from the neck.

She wasn't afraid to catch whatever it was now. If she was going to get it, she was sure she would have gotten it by now. No. God had deemed her to live in this purgatory now. Alone.

She chugged back some more of the vodka,

taking down nearly a quarter of the bottle in one go. What did it matter if she got so shit faced she couldn't see? Going through into the bedroom she picked up her backpack from beside the door and packed a few clothes into it. She didn't need much.

The world was her oyster now.

And she wasn't going to stay there. She could go anywhere. Live anywhere. Why should she stay in this shithole? It stank of melting people, as much as anything else. A bolt of sickness stabbed at her gut. Again. It was happening way too often now, and she was beginning to think that there might be something really wrong with her.

"Is there anybody there?"

Janie froze to the spot, holding a dirty t-shirt half in and half out of the bag. Fuck. What if whoever it was, was a fucking nutter? She looked around the room for a weapon. Of course she had left the knife on the flap of the drinks cabinet. She picked up the vodka bottle by the neck. It would have to do. She backed against the wall and kept still, silent.

"This is Penny Lancaster. I am broadcasting from the BBC building in London," the voice went on. Fucking hell. It was the TV. Janie dropped the bag and hurried to the living room, ignoring the copulating corpse statue. The TV signal had returned. There was a woman on there. She looked tired. Haggard, perhaps. Certainly not a news presenter. "Please, we've managed to get the signal running. Come to the BBC studio in Hackney. We're just outside of the tube station." She stopped. "Obviously that won't help. The phones are still working." She held her mobile up to the camera. "There's no reception on them, but the GPS's still work. There are more than thirty of us here. More coming. We're all women. There is no danger." She looked at the notes on the desk in front of her. "There are medical staff here. Everyone is ..." she paused, looked unsure. "We don't know what happened. We don't know what caused it, but we have food. Supplies. Even if you don't know it yet the unaffected ... we are all pregnant." She looked around unsure and someone off camera said something that Janie couldn't quiet hear. "We are all pregnant. If you are hearing this, then we believe that you are pregnant. Please. Come to the BBC studio in Hackney. If there are any men out there, even if you are unaffected, please do not approach the building. We will defend ourselves."

Janie put her hand over her belly and glanced over to Bobby. She assumed he was the glob of flesh at the back. "You're going to be a daddy," she said. She couldn't help but laugh. Fucking hell. What a way to find out.

"Please," the woman was still saying. "You are welcome here, and it is safe. We will continue this broadcast."

Janie raised her eyebrows. Hackney. Where the fuck in London was Hackney? There must also be other people—women—around here. The fucking estate was a baby factory. There must be survivors. Ones that didn't get killed by the infected. She went back to the bedroom and continued to pack her things.

It looked like she was going to have to learn how to drive a bus.

About the Author

Ash is a British horror author. He resides in the south, in the Garden of England. He writes horror that is sometimes fantastical, sometimes grounded, but always deeply graphic, and black with humour.

Printed in Great Britain
by Amazon

42745189R00051